By

Matthew B. Berg

Woodfall Press
P.O. Box #6011
Holliston, MA 01746

Copyright © 2021 Matthew B. Berg
First published in the United States by Woodfall Press
in 2020

This is a work of fiction. Names, characters, places, and
incidents either are the product of the author's
imagination or are used fictitiously, and any
resemblance to actual persons, living or dead, events, or
locales is entirely coincidental.

eBook ISBN: 0-9785791-6-X
Paperback ISBN: 979-8-59-089851-0

Printed in the United States of America
10 9 8 7 6 5 4 3 2 1

Cover art © Vivid Covers | www.VividCovers.com

STEAL THIS BOOK!

Well, you don't even have to steal it! You can get an electronic copy of it for FREE!

Claim your copy here:

https://matthewbberg.com

Join the Crafter's Guild!

Become a member and become part of the story.

- Members of the guild are always the first to hear about Matthew's new books and publications.
- Members will receive access to free behind-the-scenes content.
- Finally, some lucky guild members will have the opportunity to become beta readers for book three!

Check out the back of the book for information on how to become a guild member.

To those who have yet to discover the world of
The Crafter Chronicles . . .

*I dedicate this novelette—that you might get a
taste for what you've been missing!*

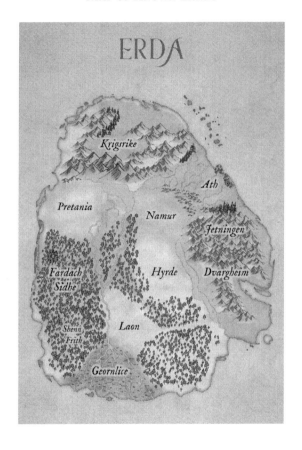

1

ENCOUNTER

There was no question that the figure was a girl. Overlapping layers of leather wrapped tightly around her slim body, narrowing at her waist, where a wide belt with three buckles secured the armor snugly over her hips. Mixed in among the pieces of leather were a few rings of chain mail, an odd steel plate, and what appeared to be stiffer segments of leather, which flared out dramatically at her shoulders. The effect of the various pieces suggested intention. These elements were not mismatched or cobbled together. Rather, they were artfully and playfully assembled, if perhaps not entirely functional.

Her hood was drawn up to conceal her features, but Oskar had a perfect angle from where she was perched to observe the soft radiance of the girl's skin and the amber glow from the center of her deep brown eyes. A few tight coils of dark hair hung down over her forehead.

The impression she made overall was stunning. If Oskar hadn't already been holding her breath, she'd likely have had it snatched from her.

Oskar was motionless. She was sure she hadn't made a sound. But the other girl's eyes suddenly shifted and bored directly into hers. Then, almost more startlingly, she raised her finger to her lips as if to enjoin Oskar to remain silent. Oskar blinked. She felt as if a giant black hole were opening at her feet and she was about to be sucked in. And then the other girl rose, turned, and leapt off the roof, out of Oskar's view. The building was three stories high! Oskar cocked her head to listen for the sound of the girl crashing to the cobbled street below. How could she hope to survive such a jump?

But no sound rose from the street. Not a rustle of cloth. It was as if the girl had never been there at all—as if the entire experience were a figment of Oskar's imagination. But the chill that washed over her body and the quiver in her spine said otherwise.

Oskar fought the urge to leave her hiding

spot, leap the alleyway, and look over the edge where the girl had disappeared.

She suddenly felt so vulnerable.

Perhaps it would be best to abort her mission for the night and simply sleep right where she was. It wouldn't be the first time she'd done that. Her body would wake up stiff in the morning. But at least she'd see morning's light. She resigned herself to doing just that. But it was a long time before sleep took her.

2

CLOSE CALL

Huw was right. Oskar was lucky. As much as she didn't want to admit it most of the time, even to herself, she was lucky.

Last night it had been that girl. That *night walker*. Her armor suggested she was a cutthroat rather than a burglar. Huw had taught Oskar that thieves should wear street clothes, so they could always blend into a crowd if needed. That girl . . . would *not* have blended in anywhere that Oskar could imagine.

And then this morning it had been the Snart brothers. She shook off a shudder and yet chuckled to herself. What a name! Huw said their name meant "pain." But they claimed it meant "quick." All Oskar knew was that they were quick, and they had caused her a good deal of pain over the years. But besides the fact that their family name sounded like *fart*, or a combination of *snot* and *fart*, Oskar only knew that they were dangerous.

This morning they had been waiting for her. Well, they didn't know she was a she. But they'd been waiting for her anyway. To work her over and take whatever she might have gotten from her haul the night before. They wouldn't know, and wouldn't believe, that she'd gotten nothing at all because her quarry had never shown. Anyway, Hugo, the tall one, was standing in the middle of the alley when she came around the corner. And curse her for a fool, she didn't think about where that sneak Wymar might be. Before she knew it, he had slipped in behind her and had his arms around her chest. That's right— her chest.

At the moment, he was probably too busy thinking about robbing her to notice that she wasn't as flat up there as she should be. Well, she was pretty flat, truth be told. But to her, the boy's hands on her chest felt like a violation. Despite the shock and surprise of the whole thing, she somehow managed to drop down and slam her elbow backward into his crotch. He let go immediately. And she bolted back the way she'd come.

Of course, she would pay for the elbow eventually. She was sure of it. But at least today she still had her own pouch of copper to show for it. Huw would probably consider it a fair trade. Coins today against Oskar's future self getting a thrashing. From the Snart boys, it would be a fair trade, anyway. As far as dwellers of the alleys of Arlon were concerned, they got much worse.

Huw was at his apple stand, right at the edge of the market district. In sight of the other, mostly more legit, hawkers selling their vegetables and fruits. They didn't like him being there, Oskar knew, because they didn't trust him. They always had to be on the lookout for him stealing from them or trying to trick them in other ways. And they also didn't like that he undercut their prices. But most of the rich folks of the city didn't make it to the "poor end" of the market district, anyway. And those who did so would rarely make it that last bit farther to visit Huw's "stand" of empty crates stacked on top of one another. Or of course, they came to him precisely because they knew what he offered that *wasn't* visible on top of the board where he displayed his apples.

Huw himself was perfectly average in height and weight. Sometimes he looked round in the belly, sometimes almost skinny. He had brown hair, a beard, and a mustache —though she'd known him to shave it all off from time to time. Today he wore the clothes of a moderately successful merchant. His tunic was embroidered in gold-colored thread, and he wore a matching box-shaped hat that made her smile. At other times, she'd known him to wear rags that would embarrass a beggar.

He was studying her in that almost disinterested way of his as she walked up. "What is it?"

She frowned. She could hide nothing from him. "Nothing."

"Clear it's not nothing. I had to guess, you had a close call not five minutes ago. You're as flushed as a maid after her first kiss!"

Huw was good.

"It was the Snart brothers." For some reason, she felt like keeping the encounter with the girl last night to herself.

"Oh." Huw just looked at her, his face entirely unreadable.

"What?"

"Nothing."

She reached over to punch him in the arm, but he pulled back in time to avoid the blow.

He smiled then.

She knew she should tell him what had happened. But she also knew that he would never ask her to do so. So she decided she would keep the tale to herself. There were few enough things in her life she had control over. Even little victories from wordplay gave her some satisfaction.

She changed the topic. "My target never showed last night."

Huw shrugged. "My sources tell me he is nearly out of material. It will be soon. Best you're up there again tonight."

Oskar felt a chill at his words. But was it fear or excitement that she was experiencing at thoughts of encountering *that girl* again? *Both*, she decided. She tried to hide her smile. Tonight couldn't come soon enough.

3

CONNECTION

"Didn't ween I'd find you here again so soon!" The girl was back. But this time, she had come up behind Oskar.

Oskar spun around to face her, her heart suddenly pounding. She was close. So close Oskar could see the knives secreted about her body. One running along each forearm. Two poking out above the top of each boot—one on the inside of each leg, and another on the outside. Interestingly enough, there were none on her belt, where an average person would wear one. Oskar guessed it might restrict her movements if she had something stiff, like a blade, at her waist.

"The person you were lurking in wait to rob last night—and are likely here again for now—is not simply a merchant, as you might think. He is also an agent of someone very powerful. I've encountered him before. Unsavory sort." She gave a smile as if to acknowledge that they could be labeled as such themselves. "You are still welcome to rob him, of course. But I'd not put myself between the wishes of a father and the defiance of his daughter if I were you. Especially when the father is your king."

"Wait . . . the princess . . . has *agents*? Isn't she a bit young to have her own spies? And why would robbing a merchant get between her and the king?"

The girl laughed then. She pitched her voice low so it wouldn't carry over the rooftops. But her laugh was rich all the same. With just the right amount of huskiness.

"The princess is hardly much older than you are. That much is true. But she has been at the game as long as I have. And I have more than a few years on you. Too, I've seen what she's capable of. And she is honing her game now. I wouldn't cross her."

"What do you mean?"

"There was the girl with the acid . . ."

"I don't know the tale."

She looked as if she'd just bitten into an apple and found a worm. "A girl spoke ill of her. She fed her a goblet of acid in retribution. Clear enough?"

Oskar shuddered. *How horrible!* "How

could even the princess get away with something like that?"

The girl's smile became more subdued. "There may be only a few years between us, and you may have grown up in these slums, but it seems you've led a sheltered life. Even the king himself would not do more than scold her for it if he knew it for a fact. But she will never dirty her own hands. There will always be distance between her and her scheming."

Oskar thought of something then, and the words came almost unbidden. "Why are you talking to me?"

The girl's smile came back. "You interest me. You are not unskilled in stealth—though your sloppiness could get you killed someday. Those two boys this morning, for example. You were too distracted to notice their trap.

"Also, I have wondered about you pretending to be a boy. It's so plain to me you are not. The way you move has no swagger. Your eyes are too soft. And your hands . . . are too delicate. Even with all your calluses."

Oskar grew pale. But the girl continued.

"So . . . to answer you properly, you have made me curious. And while I know what curiosity did to the cat, I gave in to this rare indulgence of mine because there is little in my life to make me smile. And you have already proven my instincts correct for approaching you, because here I have smiled without guile for the first time in . . . years."

"You saw me this morning?"

"I did. And those brothers who follow you sometimes. I think they suspect you are a girl as well. Or the short one does at least. But he's afraid he might be wrong and you might actually be a boy. And he doesn't want to face the consequences of knowing that truth. Better not to know than risk discovering that you are truly a boy."

Oskar's head was suddenly spinning. *Wymar suspects?* And this girl had watched her long enough to have discerned her most carefully guarded secret? Or was she just so obvious that it was plain for everyone to see? But she couldn't focus on her own problems. All she could think about was this mysterious girl. Her speech was refined and precise— like that of a member of the nobility. But she was climbing around the rooftops of the worst parts of the city at night. "Who are you?"

"No. Tonight we satisfy *my* curiosity. You must answer *my* questions about *you* first."

And so Oskar spoke. About the faint memories she had of her parents—whether those recollections were imagined or real. About her time in the orphanage. How she was thrown out for stealing. How the Begging Priest himself had found her scrounging for food and introduced her to Huw. And how Huw had raised her and looked after her after that. She also spoke about other denizens of the alleyways she called home. The Snart brothers. The girls she'd met who had come and gone too quickly. Her unpleasant guesses at their fates. And finally, about meeting one girl up on the rooftops— who already seemed to know too much about Oskar before she'd even shared her story.

Oskar tried again when she had finished. "But who are *you*?"

The girl smiled broadly. "Next time!" And then she was moving.

She dropped over the edge of the roof right before Oskar's eyes. But this time, Oskar had the opportunity to watch. And it was even more impressive than when Oskar had thought the girl must possess some type of magic. Her fingers caught the lip of the roof at the last moment. Then she sprang across the alley to a windowsill one story below, then back to the building Oskar was on, and again across the alley. In moments, the girl was standing on the alley floor—over thirty feet below. She looked up briefly and made eye contact with Oskar. And then she made the turn around the corner and was gone.

4

SILVER

After the girl left her, Oskar's target
finally appeared. She tracked him from
the rooftop until she confirmed the route he
was taking, and then she worked her way
down to the street—albeit not as quickly as
the girl had. From there the theft was almost
disappointingly easy. She accidentally
bumped into the man, apologized, and then
ran away with his case in hand before he'd
even properly registered that it was gone. She
knew the streets in a way he didn't. He had no
chance of catching up to her.

Once she reached her nearest hiding
place—Huw called them "holes"—a couple
of streets over, she took the time to transfer
the contents of the man's case to a simple
leather sack she had brought with her for
the purpose. She also removed her home-

spun tunic and left it in the hole. She was wearing a finer, blue tunic underneath. Then she donned a matching blue cap and made her way back to the location where Huw had told her they should meet. His stall at the market was his public meeting place, where people might expect to find him if they hadn't made other arrangements. But he had a number of these other safe places around the city. She was aware of at least half a dozen he'd used recently, and two more he'd abandoned over the years. She figured he was probably always finding new places to lie low.

He was just where he'd told her he would be. And he was pleased with her success.

"Very good. The silversmith doesn't trust anyone else to buy his stock for him. He's always thought the delivery boys were skimming a portion of the silver they were supposed to be bringing to him. He was right, of course!" Huw laughed. "But I can't have him depriving those boys, not to mention the local economy."

Oskar watched Huw in silence for a moment as he carefully emptied out the bars, rods, and spools of wire. All made of pure silver.

He looked up at her and seemed to read something in her expression. "Okay . . . I let it go yesterday, but I'm not letting you leave here until you tell me what's going on."

She frowned. His ability to read her was unreal. "I had an encounter."

Huw sat up straighter. "Go on."

"She was dressed all in black. Armored in tight-fitting leather, with shoulder guards and steel accent pieces. No cloak or loose fabric. Blades in her boots and on her forearms. And the way she moved! She practically flowed to the ground from the rooftop. Was she an assassin?"

Huw was thoughtful. "A woman, you say. Unusual. Did she see you?"

Oskar had the grace to look embarrassed as she responded. "Well . . . I talked to her."

Huw's face became deadly serious, and he put down the spool of wire in his hand. "I'm sorry?"

"We talked. She . . . said she's been watching me. In fact, I saw her the other night as well, though we didn't talk then. But last night . . . she knew I was . . . she knew my secret."

"What?"

"It's okay. She never threatened me. Or made me feel in any danger. In fact . . . she told me she's seen the Snart brothers following me before. And she warned me about getting between the princess and the king."

Huw whistled low and leaned back. "Well, this tale is getting stranger by the moment. I don't know what to say. Did she say who she worked for?"

Oskar shook her head.

It took Huw longer than usual to compose himself. But once he did, it seemed he'd run through a list in his head and was happy with his own calculations.

"If she, or her employer, wanted you dead . . . you'd be dead. Yes?"

With no false modesty or hesitation, Oskar nodded her head. "For certain. I've never seen anyone move like her before."

Huw shook his head.

"By your description of her armor, I'd say she is well funded. That alone is enough to give me pause. And the way you describe her movement makes me think of someone trained in the shadow arts of Namur. I haven't heard anything about shadow walkers being active in the city. But they generally don't tie themselves to factions. They tend to operate independently—at least in their homeland. That could be good news for you too—unless she considers you part of her mission somehow, of course, and she intends to use you for her own ends.

"And of course, if she's been following you, there's a better-than-even chance she knows about me as well. Damn me, but I've been living down on the streets too long. I'm like the rat in the alley, digging in the garbage for his dinner, that doesn't see the owl's shadow overhead. Thank the gods I have you up on the rooftops! I'd never have seen this coming.

"Well . . . I certainly hope I've taught you well enough that I don't need to warn you to be careful around her. But if you do encounter her again, try to figure out what you can about her job. It's almost certain she'll tell you nothing. But then, I think we're already in unmapped territory here."

5

STREET WORK

The next day, Oskar had no plans, so she decided to join Huw at his stand. He'd always told her she was a natural at talking people out of their money, and that she shouldn't think she was going to be climbing about on rooftops for the rest of her life. But to Oskar, tricking people face-to-face felt less honest than climbing through their windows and stealing from them while they slept. The latter was cleaner. No need to look them in the eye. No faces to recall in her dreams, making her relive the guilt. But still, she had to admit that doing things Huw's way was often an easier way to put food on the table. And if you did it right, the victim wouldn't even know they'd been tricked. Plus nobody would try to hunt you down to get their money back.

She looked up and realized that Huw had been watching her with a questioning look on his face. "What is it now?"

But Huw said nothing and lifted his chin a touch to indicate that Oskar should look behind her.

She turned around and saw a young man approaching their stall. *Ah. A dupe!*

Oskar knew that sitting back and waiting for your target to come to you was a sure way to go home empty-handed. You needed to offer up a fish to get the gull's attention. She stepped out in front of the stall and approached the boy.

"Good morning! My name is Oskar. Are you new to the city?"

He seemed surprised to be approached. But his eyes lit up a bit at the attention. "Why, yes. I'm from a small village to the west. You've probably never heard of it before."

"Try me."

"It's Eaweald."

"Eaweald? You don't say! Do you live in the forest or down by the river?"

"You know it! Well, I never would have thought anyone here would know of it. I live down by the river. Upstream from the tanner, of course."

Oskar laughed at the joke. Tanners were famous for fouling the waters below their shops. But if the boy was talking about living *above* the tanner, he was probably poor enough that he felt it important to make the distinction. Oh well, no nobleman's purse from this one. But a copper was a copper. "Well, you look successful enough—for a lad from the country. First off, tell us your name. Then let us know what brings you here and how we can help you."

"My name is Tad. And I've come to find my father."

"Is he lost, then? Who was supposed to be watching him?"

Tad gave Oskar a somewhat vacant stare.

Oskar offered Huw a quick glance to let him know that she felt good about their chances with this one. And then she clued the young man in on her jest. "I was just joking. I'm sorry. Is it a sad tale that brings you to us? Your spirits seem high enough I'd never have thought you were here with bad news."

"Oh. That's funny! I get it now. No, he's not lost, exactly. He just left my ma and me when I was little."

"Little, eh? And how old are you now, then?"

"I'm fifteen."

"Fifteen! Same as me!" Truth be told, Oskar wasn't exactly sure how old she was. But she thought she could pass for fifteen.

She continued. "So, how do you plan to find your da, then? And what makes you think he's still here? You sure you're not on a fool's errand?" Oskar knew that it was easier to get someone to trust you if you challenged them or tested them in some way. Even the most gullible rustic might catch on if you were too friendly. But as strange as it seemed, people tended to trust you more when you gave them a little grief to win their trust.

Tad's smile did fade a bit. But it brightened when he spoke next. "He was a fletcher. The best for leagues around. But he told my ma he'd never make his fortune out in the middle of nowhere, and he'd have to go to the city, where his talents would prove more valuable. He said he'd come back once he'd made his fortune. But that was years ago now."

"A fletcher! A noble trade, that! Nothing worse than an arrow that won't fly true. And your ma knows you're here? She let you come here alone to find him?"

"Actually, she's dead. A fever took her a few weeks ago. She was delirious at the end. Talked about my father in ways I'd never heard before. Called him a rascal. And worse. But she'd never spoken an ill word about him in my whole life before. Must have been the fever talking."

The tale was becoming clearer to Oskar.

"If he was a fletcher, surely he must have found his way to the King's Army, then, no?"

"Yes. That's where I started. But the men working for the king's fletcher didn't know who I was talking about. Hadn't ever met a man of my father's description."

Oskar's interest was waning in the tale. *How can I turn this into an opportunity to make money?* Plus she already knew that Tad was unlikely to provide much in the way of coin, no matter how elaborate a story she concocted. So she decided to cut the line on this one.

"If the fletchers working for the army have never heard of your da, I'd say there's a good chance he never came here. Maybe the tale he told your ma, or the tale she told you, was nothing but a kind yarn to protect you from the truth. That your da had met another woman. Or he ended up in an almshouse here in the city. Or worse. I'm sorry, lad. But I'm afraid this story may not end the way you hope."

Huw coughed behind her. She glanced back to see him giving her a quizzical look. But she just didn't have the heart to take advantage of this one. The chances were good he'd never find his father. And she couldn't bring herself to use his pain to make a few coins for herself. She turned back. Tad looked ready to burst into tears.

"Come with me. I'll take you to the Begging Priest. If anyone can help you find your father, it's him. No matter what's happened to him or where he's gone. If he did come to the city, that is."

Oskar put her arm around the young man and looked back at Huw, offering him a shrug. What did he expect her to do? Heap on the boy's troubles by robbing him blind?

6

THE SNART BROTHERS

This time it was Hugo who got his hands on her when she took a tight corner on one of her usual routes to check in with Huw. Maybe she wasn't always lucky. Her captor crossed his thigh in front of him to prevent her from effecting the same escape she'd managed from his brother the day before. Hugo was strong. And he was a good deal taller, and broader of shoulder, than his brother, Wymar. He always handled her a bit more roughly too. So she was actually glad that it was Wymar doing the hitting while Hugo held her still.

The first punch was right in the center of her gut. It knocked the wind out of her and caused her to bend forward quickly. Which, of course, led to the second punch being an uppercut to her chin. Her teeth slammed together so hard she smelled something like smoke from the impact. Still, if it had been Hugo, he may have shattered some teeth with the same blow. *I am grateful for even the smallest blessings*—as the Begging Priest would always say when she dropped a copper in his bowl.

Hugo adjusted his grip and was now holding her arms behind her like a butcher dressing a hen. She could see Wymar's face shift from one thought to another while he calculated his next strike. He hesitated for a moment longer. And then he swung a wide, arcing blow toward her face. She turned her head just as his fist struck, and he caught her a solid clout on her cheek. *That will leave a mark.*

He watched for her reaction, hesitated another second, and then he nodded to his brother. "Okay. That's enough for now. But there's more where that came from if you don't listen good to our offer."

What had she gotten herself into now?

"So here is the plan . . . We need you to steal something for us. We'd get it ourselves, you see, except that you are a better climber than I am. And Hugo here is afraid of heights."

Hugo raised her arms higher behind her, causing her to flinch.

"I'm going to need my arms if you expect me to climb somewhere for you."

Wymar nodded to Hugo, and he lowered her arms slightly—not back to where they'd been a moment before, but at least it made her feel as though the possibility that both her shoulders would pop out of their sockets at the same time had diminished somewhat.

"What's the job?"

Wymar seemed suddenly happier. "Excellent. It's a downright *noble* job. Trust us! And there'll even be a few swans in it for you if you succeed. A few for you and a few for us, of course. Swans for a *crown*, if you will! And since you're such a *royal* pain in the arse, it's the perfect job for you."

If Oskar hadn't been at risk of having her arms torn off, she'd have told Wymar that he could have stopped at the first pun. *Yup. I've got it, Wymar. The job is for a noble—and maybe even someone important at that, like the king!*

"You need to steal us a letter."

That didn't sound so bad. "From where?"

"Some lord's house. In the Laonese Quarter. The letter will be addressed to Lord Tobryn Langwen of Reinne and bear the king's seal. It grants him entitlements the king no longer wishes to confer. Rather than go back on his word, he asked us to retrieve the letter and return it to him. But since we also can't read, we need you to get it for us. Oh, and our patron made it very clear that you're to steal *nothing else* while you are in there."

"Okay. I've got it. You can let go of me now."

Instead, Hugo raised Oskar's arms higher. Oskar felt a sharp burn in her left shoulder blade. And then Hugo released her abruptly with a rough shove. She stumbled to the ground, her numbed arms failing to respond quickly enough to stop her from tumbling to the dirt.

"Get on with it, then! Or I'll have worse to do to you . . . later!" The words were rough and clumsy, like the oversize boy who had thrown her to the ground. But the message was as strong as he was. If she didn't do this job for them, they'd find her eventually. And the price for her disobedience, as always, would be pain.

Huw watched his apprentice approach. He saw the girl beneath the artfully applied soot and the roughly cut bangs of her hair, beneath the shapeless clothing that wouldn't attract attention anywhere outside a royal court. But he knew that most people couldn't see what he saw. Nor many other things that were right before their eyes—until you gave them a reason to see them. The wife who chose not to notice the little signs that her husband was cheating on her. The father who convinced himself that there must be another explanation for his losses than his son slowly stealing away his savings. Seeing beyond what one expected required effort most people didn't care to muster.

Not *her* hair, then. *His.* Huw needed to remember that Oskar was playing a role. If he thought of her as a boy and treated her as such, it would sell her ruse better to Oskar herself, as well as anyone who might chance to be watching.

Oskar didn't waste any time, in that way of *his*. "Wymar kept saying 'royal this' and 'noble that' about the job. Clearly, he is proud of the fact that somebody important hired them for this one."

Huw tried to figure out what he was talking about. But Oskar had a way of starting a tale in the middle, as if he didn't have the resolve to tell the whole tale from the beginning but assumed you were smart enough to figure it out as he continued. It was both flattering and exasperating at the same time. As much as Huw liked to puzzle out Oskar's stories in his own time, he didn't have the patience today.

"Who now? The Snarts have been hired for a job? What's that to you, then?"

"Well . . ."

Huw knew that look. He had taught Oskar to hold things back—even from him. That keeping one's own secrets was the best practice for keeping those of others. But again, he didn't have the forbearance today. "Out with it!"

Oskar looked at him with that vaguely

hurt look of hers . . . *his*. Huw could never tell whether that look was real or assumed. But he didn't care right now.

"Tell me."

Oskar's shoulders slumped. "They caught me this time. And made me swear I'd do a job for them. They want me to steal a letter from someone in the Laonese Quarter."

Huw frowned. "Why them? Who thought the Snart brothers would be good candidates for it? They're as like to botch it as not. Does that suggest to you that whoever arranged for this stolen letter might not *want* them to succeed? And do you think even the brothers were smart enough to figure that out, so that's why they asked *you* to do it? And none of that even addresses the fact that they can't read to know one letter from another!"

Huw lowered his voice and muttered to himself then, as much as to Oskar. "Is this a chess game we are talking about? Or someone's throw of the dice?" And then he continued, once again making it clear he was talking to Oskar.

"Well . . . if there's even a chance that the king is really involved, then I think you need to do it. And hope that it's not a trick of some kind, because it's not so far a stretch to think the king might come to learn the truth, that you've done the work. And that could lead to better opportunities for you down the road.

"Meanwhile, I'll look into this Laonese nobleman and see what I can learn about him. What's his name, then?"

"Lord Tobryn Langwen of Reinne."

AFTER OSKAR LEFT, it didn't take Huw long to find what he sought. And the news wasn't good. It *was* the king who had arranged for the theft that Oskar was going to attempt that night. But someone else wanted this Lord Tobryn Langwen to retain his honors. Someone with power that sought to rival the king's own. And while Huw's spy had his guesses about who that might be, he knew that his man up the chain of command to the king had made it abundantly clear: the king wanted to send a message. He would not tolerate his bannermen splitting their loyalties. There would be consequences if someone tried to interfere with his plans.

So if it was so important, why send the Snart boys?

I need to find Oskar and tell him to be exceptionally careful tonight—if he hasn't already left.

But as much as Huw wanted to be sure his disciple was safe, he knew that it wasn't just Oskar who was in danger. The contests among the lords and ladies of Arlon were starting up again and becoming more serious. And when the houses clashed, and the smell of blood was in the air, the carrion feeders would descend upon his city—if they hadn't already.

8

DAUGHTER'S TALE

"My name is Nia—though none would call me that here."

Oskar had feared she would never see the mysterious shadow walker again. But the girl had found her on the roof that night as she was headed toward the Laonese Quarter, where she would be stealing the letter for the Snart brothers.

Oskar hadn't even noticed her. The girl's words had come out of the darkness. Oskar stopped walking and sat down. She felt safer when her bottom was resting on the slates of the roof, with her feet below her. The girl stood calmly and confidently between Oskar and the edge, as if she were standing firmly on the ground below.

She continued. "My father was a healer. He

expected me to learn his craft, and he trained me as his assistant from a very young age. Most of what I studied involved simple cures that every hedge witch in Erda knows. Balms, analeptics . . . poisons. But I learned some real medicine too. From gauging the effect of a potion by feeling for the blood pump at a man's wrist or neck, to cutting open a festering wound in order to drain it and dress it with a poultice, to tying off the leg of a man bitten by a venomous spider. Sawing off a limb. Burning what remains to stop the bleeding. Better to lose a leg than die a slow death of rot and pain.

"I was never squeamish. And over time, I became more and more accustomed to the dissection, the smell of an opened body or of burned flesh. I discovered that we are little different from the dogs and suckling pigs we roast over our fires. Our muscles and bones, and even our organs, seemed the same to me. Just with slightly different configurations. That was a beginning.

"I saw wild pigs rooting among the decaying filth in our refuse heap. That was the day I stopped eating meat.

"My father drank potions every day to balance his humors. I took up the habit as well. But for what reason, I cannot say . . . because death had lost its grip on me."

Oskar was mesmerized. She had so many questions already. But the girl continued.

"A man once asked my father for poison, and he wouldn't sell it to him. He told the man to return the next day, when his choler had subsided. He would sell him the poison then if he still wanted it. I gave the man a signal as he left, and I met him afterward with a vial of the liquid he had asked for. He paid me well.

"That was the first death for which I was directly responsible. Well, the first two deaths. The man's wife from the poison, and then the man himself the next day—when our prince learned of him murdering his wife. She had been the prince's own daughter."

Nia paused for a moment and looked up at the stars overhead. And then she continued. "I do not tell you these things to excuse my actions, and the decisions I have made, but rather to explain to you who I am, that my life may serve as a lesson for you. You were free enough in telling me your story. I have thought about it all day. Considered your circumstances. The decisions you yourself have faced and made.

"You are a thief. At times, you steal from those who are nearly as unfortunate as you are. You justify your actions to yourself because you feel you must do so to survive. Your childhood has been hard. It was you or it was them. Perhaps I have misjudged you in these matters. But I think not.

"For me, I never wanted for anything. I always had comfortable clothes, shoes on my feet, and a belly full of healthy food. Even when I stopped eating meat, there were always plenty of fresh fruits and vegetables to fill me up. And endless grain.

"Yet in some ways it is true that you are lucky, as you tell me Huw is always saying. And it is certainly the case that you do not want to be as I am.

"Maybe I never had it. Perhaps I lost it somewhere along the way. But I do not feel compassion. Even for you, who perhaps could have become my friend—if our circumstances had been different.

"It may hurt you to hear it, but as things are, you are at most a curiosity to me. A nostalgic view into a *me* I could have been, perhaps. In another life. Free to move about the city. To squeak when you are frightened. To redden when you admire a boy. Free to leave Arlon if you should choose to do so.

"If I were in your place, I am certain I would leave these alleys and rooftops behind. I see by the look on your face that you already acknowledge it to yourself. You do not belong in this world.

"My choices, if I ever had any, were to learn my father's craft or to wander off into the open plains—where I would not have survived.

"I resented my father for what he did to me. So on the day he died, I broke free from his orbit. I took the tools I had learned at his side, and I tried to set my own course. But mine became a dark road. No better than his in many ways. And worse in perhaps the most important way: mine was a path without mercy. He would have been appalled at what I have become."

Nia stopped talking, and Oskar got the impression she had said what she'd wanted to.

Oskar spoke to fill the void. "I never knew my parents. But I like to think they loved me. I am sorry your father was not kind to you. Did you . . . have a mother?" Oskar wasn't trying to be cruel. If she was honest with herself, she was hoping for a happier tale about Nia's mother. A tale of a good parent. A story of someone who, per-haps, fought for her daughter. Loved and cared for her child.

Nia's face had been flat when she'd told her story. She smiled now. But the smile was sadder than when she had been so serious moments before. She simply shook her head.

Oskar wasn't sure what the gesture was supposed to tell her. No, she'd never had a mother? No, she didn't have a happy tale to tell of a mother? But she guessed that the smile and the lack of a story were a kindness of sorts. She guessed that the truth would only share an even greater sadness.

Nia surprised Oskar then by speaking again.

"My father talked of our people coming across the Eastern Sea many generations ago —and settling in Namur. He spoke of the vast plains here being kind and forgiving, while the sands of our home long ago were not so benevolent. He talked of the lessons taught by a desert.

"He said that we are weak. That we have forgotten. That focus and patience and will were forged in our desert. And that we are lessened every day we live in this land of plenty. But I think that those who are born here, in this soft place, are lucky. *You* are lucky. Life can be so much worse even than the one you have led, Oskar."

Neither of them spoke after that. The silence grew between them. But it was a comfortable silence. A shared moment between two people who desperately needed each other, but who both knew they would never be more than two strangers who sometimes met on the darkened rooftops of Arlon.

Oskar felt the moment stretch and then begin to fade. And the tension began to build within her to move again. "I should go. I have a job to do."

Nia smiled again. Still sad, but slightly less so this time. "Then by all means, please proceed. And be cautious . . . There are dark magics abroad tonight."

9

THE JOB

Oskar rarely visited the Laonese Quarter. But she liked the feel of the place. In the poorer part of the district, it was loud and boisterous, with music spilling out through the doorways of the taverns. Singing —among the patrons as much as the hired musicians. Flutes. Stringed instruments. And the smells of spicy food wafting out along with the music. Her senses were filled with . . . *comfort*, she realized. It was a welcoming and embracing combination of sights, sounds, and smells. And it dispelled Nia's words of dark magics, which had trapped a shiver inside her.

All the homes along the main roadway had balconies on their second stories, running the entire width of the houses. The columns and railings would make it easy enough to climb up to the roof of any one of them. But the residents liked to sit out under the stars all through the night. And tonight's moon was high and bright enough that its light nearly seemed like daylight, even without any of the myriad lanterns everywhere she looked. Darkness wouldn't be driving these people to their beds anytime soon.

The sounds of the inhabitants were continuous. The clinking of glasses and the hollow clunk of wooden mugs. The shouting down to passersby—and across the street. Encouraging the rare unaccompanied female to come on up and join them. Hurling the occasional insult. And laughing. Lots of raucous laughing.

Oskar left the laughter and music behind as she worked her way toward the more staid district of the Laonese Quarter, where the wealthier residents lived. When she finally reached the house of her target, the sounds of the poorer district were a distant memory. The low coos of roosting doves and the muffled voices from inside one of the nearby homes were the only sounds here.

Lord Tobryn Langwen's house was immense. It had a large portico in front, where a carriage could pick up and dispense passengers out of the weather. Unlike the earlier houses she had passed, this home had no balcony. But the columns supporting the portico made it easy enough for her to scramble up onto the roof just the same.

When she reached the roof, she imagined she was the assassin—making her moves even stealthier than she normally did, creeping along the ridge of the roof. She pretended in that moment that she was on an errand to kill a merciless criminal—and not simply purloin a letter.

She wouldn't have been able to tell from the street, but the house was framed around a large courtyard in its center. Trees grew up from inside. And one even reached the height of the roof. *Convenient!*

She leapt from the roof onto a broad branch, shimmied down the trunk, and was safely on the grass of the courtyard in a few seconds. She smiled. *The shadow walker could hardly have managed better!*

She held herself still in the moon-cast shadows of the tree for a long moment, mastering her breathing and scanning the area for any signs she'd been seen.

She saw no movement anywhere. And she could hear nothing. There was no wind to blow the tops of the trees here. And no sound of the doves she'd heard from the street. The silence was more complete than it ever got back in her neighborhood. There was a ceaseless succession of clattering, shuffling, and shouting from near and far away back among her alleyways. Here it was so quiet it was starting to make her uneasy. She knew from experience that movement helped calm her down, so she shook off another shiver and decided to just get on with it.

She braced herself and walked slowly toward the darkest corner of the yard. She scanned around, trying to identify where she should enter the home. Expensive glass windows looked in on the courtyard from all four sides. But there were no lamps lit within. She would have to rely on the moonlight to aid her. One window revealed a room containing a table with two chairs next to a long couch. Another was so dark that it defied her ability to see inside. And the third . . . was a library! Dozens of books lined the walls on ornately carved wooden shelves. That would be a good place to look for a letter.

As she turned toward the nearest door, her foot caught on something in the grass, likely a rock, and she tumbled, catching herself from falling flat only by virtue of placing her hand on the ground to steady herself. She could feel her face flush despite the fact that she was alone in the dark.

She stood awkwardly, quietly wiped the moisture from her hand, and felt the tension rise within her as she made her way, more slowly now, toward the door. She had brought a set of picks with her to open any locks she might face. It was not her strength though. She often struggled with any lock beyond the most basic. Huw, on the other hand, could pick a lock in his sleep. For the hundredth time, she wondered at whether there was some other path she could take. She wasn't sure she was cut out for burglary. She tried the handle. Unlocked! *Ah. Another obstacle overcome!*

Huw had taught her to read. She had mostly practiced with the Begging Priest's book of prayers. But the calligraphy of the scribes who had produced the prayer book was far superior to the penmanship used by merchants and nobility. So despite the Snart brothers having chosen her for this job because she could read, she was concerned she wouldn't recognize the document when she found it.

There was a small writing desk in one corner of the room. She started there, rummaging through the dozens of drawers and behind tiny doors that mostly seemed to hold writing supplies and other odds and ends. There was a beautiful statue of a stork, carved from a wood she didn't recognize. She picked it up and ran her thumb across the finely worked feathers of its wing. The surface of the wood seemed almost oily. She briefly considered taking the bird as a souvenir. But the Snart brothers had been clear that the theft was a message, and she wasn't to confuse matters by stealing anything else. She did not fear them. But she didn't know what the others involved might think about the missing bird. For all she knew, it held special meaning for this Langwen fellow. She carefully placed it back where she'd found it, and she continued her search. But the desk revealed nothing.

Where else . . . ? She scanned the room again. Between the shelves, on a narrow section of wall by the window, was a document in a frame. *Could it be that obvious?* She moved closer. It was too dark for her to see it clearly, but there appeared to be a seal on it. She removed the frame from the wall and held it up to the window to catch what moonlight was available. This could be it. Below the illegible signature at the bottom was the word "king." And the top used a lot of words with which she was unfamiliar. But she caught "Langwen," "grant," and "titles." *This must be it!*

She examined the way the vellum had been stretched into the edges of the frame. She would rather not carry this bulky frame away with her. It would hamper her movements. So she pulled out a flat-tipped blade she carried in her kit for prying and slipping latches, and she quickly disassembled the entire frame, freeing the vellum from the wood. It curled slightly as she released it from its restraints, so she worked with the natural curl of the scraped hide and rolled it into a tube, which she then tucked into her belt. *Much better.*

Within a few minutes, she was out the door, up the tree, and back on the roof of the home. If she had been in the city proper, she'd have been able to leap from one building to another. But out here she'd need to sprout wings to make such a jump. The homes were huge, and the lands surrounding them were even more expansive. *Imagine owning a piece of land as vast as this.* Not only did she not have a true home, but she rarely slept in the same place every night. And the whole idea of owning *land*, never mind having enough possessions to fill the empty spaces of one's own *library* . . . She could carry everything she owned in a medium-sized sack. And she was prepared to walk away from even those few things if she had to. And she'd had to—more times than she cared to count.

The moon was still up and providing enough light that she realized she was probably giving anyone nearby an excellent view of her profile against the sky. She decided she'd better get down off this mansion and return to the relative safety of the streets and alleys of the Laonese Quarter.

10

SHADOWS

S he was nearly back to the comfort of her own territory. And she had started to relax and let down her guard a bit. Nobody had followed her from the Laonese Quarter. She was sure of it. But Huw had ever cautioned her to be extra vigilant when she found herself feeling safe. So rather than continuing to walk at ground level, she had taken to the rooftops again once the buildings became crowded enough, or more accurately, once the alleyways she'd have to jump across were narrow enough to allow it.

She could see the lantern in front of the King's Mercy tavern. That corner marked the edge of where Huw had always told her she would be safe. The area beyond was his. He had paid, in coin, barter, and blood, to hold it.

And for as long as she'd known it, it had proven safe, as promised.

The light from the lantern dimmed momentarily and then became bright again, as if a cloth had been placed over it and then removed. Not like normal cloth, but rather like the fine veils she'd seen on wealthy noblewomen. She focused on the lantern itself and noticed that there was a ripple of movement in the air in front of her. Not quite a veil. More like the air above a flame. She could see through it. But everything beyond seemed slightly twisted out of shape.

She slowed her pace. What ill fate was befalling her now? She briefly considered backtracking. But the rooftops ahead of her had no openings where someone could hide. No crates. Not even a chimney. Just a straight run to the corner that marked the boundary of Huw's dominion. But she couldn't ignore that . . . *warping* in the air. Caution made her walk farther to the left, away from the edge.

She had nearly reached the place where the air was *wrong*. The hairs on the back of her neck had begun to rise, and she quickened her pace again. She had been straining her eyes so hard that they were drying out. She blinked. Just for a second. And then there was a man suddenly standing to her right. He had bronze skin. And he was as gaunt as a beggar. But he was no pauper. His clothes were all of dark blue silk or satin. And they were in a style she'd never seen before. A very short jacket. A sash around his waist. And baggy pants. His hair ruined the impression made by his fine clothes, however. It was black and greasy and plastered to his head.

He reached out, his hand extending a short rod in her direction. The tip nearly came in contact with her cheek, but she managed to drop to the roof and roll away from him. She came to a stop right at the roof's edge.

She'd hardly even registered the fact that her body had reacted more quickly than her wits likely would have. And she was grateful to discover that she'd even rolled in the right direction—toward the King's Mercy. She shifted her weight to stand, and the piece of slate under her left foot cracked and gave way. She fell hard onto her elbow, while both of her feet and most of her body slid off the edge and were now hanging in open space. She was bearing all of her weight on her left forearm. Her right hand had instinctively grabbed onto her left wrist. She tried to let go and find a grip to pull herself up. But there was nothing to grab onto. Just downward-sloping slates.

She chanced a look up toward her pursuer. He was walking quickly down the slope of the roof toward her—not running, but walking at a measured pace that would bring him to her within a handful of seconds. He slowly extended the wand in his hand as he came nearer.

Oskar tried one last time to find a way to shift her weight or gain some purchase. It just wasn't going to happen. She glanced behind her. *Is there any way . . . ? There!* A waterspout on the opposite wall of the alley. Nia would have leapt backward and nimbly latched onto the drainpipe. Oskar didn't like her chances. But the gods only knew what would happen to her if that man reached her.

She tried to get her feet on the wall beneath her, but she was dangling too far out on the overhang. She would have to drop first and then try to push off the wall. And if she couldn't manage it, she'd be falling thirty feet straight down to the cobblestones. The man stepped closer, slowing down as he reached nearer to the edge of the roof. Her time was up.

She let go.

As she fell, she tried to maintain her orientation, to keep her sense of up and down. She felt her toes touch something solid and pushed off from it as hard as she could— hoping it was the nearer wall, and praying to

Mungo that she was pushing herself toward the opposite side of the alley and the drainpipe that represented her only hope of stopping her fall. She tried to spin her body and keep the drainpipe in sight. Her right hand touched it. The weathered bronze was rougher than she'd thought it would be, and she managed to grab on. Her hand slid around the back of the pipe, and she brought her left arm up to grab on as well. But the weight of her body was dragging her downward, and her hands slid down the pipe.

And then her wrists encountered one of the straps that held the pipe to the wall. The force of all her weight came to bear on both of her wrists as they struck the sturdy piece of metal. Her vision went black for a moment from the intensity of the pain, and her hands opened of their own accord.

Instinct made her cradle her head in her battered arms as she fell the remaining twenty feet or so to the alley floor. She hit hard, the balls of both feet striking the ground at nearly the same time. Her overbalanced body crumpled backward from the impact, and her knees bent so far behind her she felt the heels of her boots dig into the back of her thighs. And then she was on her back, with her legs twisted awkwardly behind her.

She lay still. In shock at what had happened. How quickly she had fallen from the height of confidence she'd been feeling from a job done well. To a broken thing lying in filth in an alley. She was looking up at the narrow band of sky above her. The man was leaning over the rooftop, looking down at her, his face shrouded in darkness, his silhouetted figure blacker than the darkness of the sky behind him. He watched her for a long moment before he finally stepped back from the edge.

Oskar hadn't tried to move yet—not because she was feigning injury for the man's sake, but because she feared discovering that she couldn't move at all, feared learning what injuries awaited her when she tried to use her body. She tried rolling to her left. Rolling should be safe. Her left arm protested. Badly. There was a piercing pain in her elbow, and her left wrist was severely bruised, or worse. Altogether the arm wouldn't bear her weight to stand.

She tried rolling in the other direction. Her right wrist was sore, but not as bad as her left. It bore her weight as she tried to stand. Her knees protested, and she felt a searing pain in her hips as she stood to her full height. But she could bear it. Miraculously, she realized, she could walk.

She smiled grimly. Nia might very well have been horrified at her lack of grace, but she had survived the fall. Now she needed to find someplace safe to hide as quickly as she could before that *man* made his way down to the streets and found her.

11

MISSING

She wasn't sure she would ever feel safe on the rooftops again. What had once been her haven now reeked of violation. So she slept in another one of the holes that were shared among anyone who needed a safe spot to stay for a few hours or days in the maze of alleyways that made up the poor section of Arlon. Who was that man? What dark magic did he command that had kept him hidden from her? And why had he attacked her? She'd only had a few proper baths in her life, but her encounter had her thinking she'd welcome that cruel lye soap Huw had made her use that time she'd gotten fleas. *Such horrid little things.* Fortunately, as a boy, the extreme haircut she'd gotten at the hands of Huw hadn't even raised an eyebrow among her friends on the street.

In comparison with what had just happened to her, she'd have welcomed a flea bath. Her body was so sore. Her hips ached, and her right wrist was tender. But her left arm felt like it might be broken. She rigged up a simple sling for herself. She had done so many times before, as a prop when she was playing at begging or working on some other deceit. It surprised her how much it actually helped to bear the weight of her injured arm and ease the pain.

She would have to visit the Begging Priest and make a donation. If there was a single god up there who had created everything, surely He could manage to keep her safe from that evil spawn of a man who had chased her last night. She felt a chill between her shoulder blades, and she gave an involuntary shudder. *Dark magics. He must be a sorcerer of some kind.*

But first things first. She had to find Huw —to tell him what had happened, and see what he might be able to find out. She checked the usual places, starting with his stall. Huw moved around when necessary, so she wasn't overly alarmed when he wasn't where he'd told her he would be. She looked for any sign that he might have been there. Nothing appeared out of order. He could have been there an hour earlier or not have been there for weeks. That was his way. To leave no trace.

She checked all of the usual places, even roaming beyond their usual haunts. Nothing. Nobody had heard from him.

She had almost given up, and was ready to head back to his stall to wait for him, when she came upon a crowd of people gathered around the entrance to an alley just outside her territory. She recognized a few of the faces, so she edged her way into the group to see what had caught their attention.

A crumpled form lay on the ground, and a second figure lay several feet away. Her heart rose into her throat. *Huw!* But then someone nudged the smaller of the two bodies to turn it over, and she could see the face. *Wymar!* The light had gone from his eyes, and his features were grey, ashen. While there was no obvious sign of injury or blood, it was clear he was dead. Did that make the other body Hugo's? She pushed through the crowd and rushed over to check. *Yes.* It was Hugo. Like his brother, he bore no obvious injury. His eyes were vacant and his skin was ashen as well.

She looked around. Were there other bodies? Was it just the Snart brothers? It seemed to be. What should she do with the letter now? *And where is Huw?*

12

THE BEGGING PRIEST

Something caught Oskar's eye as she approached the Begging Priest's stall. It was a cat, and it looked to be in a precarious position. It was perched on the narrow sill of a closed window at least ten feet above the Begging Priest's head. The cat appeared trapped up there, as Oskar could see no obvious way down. Yet as she approached, the animal casually dropped off the ledge and flowed down the side of the brick wall. Its paws maintained contact with the vertical surface of the wall as confidently as Oskar might use a set of stairs. It landed gently on the alley floor and calmly walked over to the priest, arching its back up and against his elbow. The priest smiled and idly ran his hand down the cat's back.

Oskar was impressed. That cat might

even have a *slight* edge on Nia. But she wasn't sure. One thing she did know was that she'd never be capable of moving like that. Maybe Nia had undergone years of training and preparation. But Oskar knew that natural talent must come into play for her as well.

Some days, Oskar felt okay about her abilities. She was usually *good enough* at being a thief. She could steal from the average victim without much effort. But she'd never be great. Not in the way that cat so naturally found footholds among the protruding bricks of a vertical wall. Not in the way Nia was. And certainly not against adversaries as dangerous as the sorcerer she'd encountered the night before.

She fought off a shiver at the memory. But she couldn't shake off the truth. This life just wasn't for her. She hated to admit it about herself, but she would need to stop scampering around on rooftops and find a way to survive down on the streets themselves. Where the people were. And where she'd always thought most of the danger was. Until now. Because if there was anything the past few weeks had taught her, it was that she didn't belong on the rooftops, as dangerous as the game was on the street. She knew that the players on the rooftops were hunters. And she was prey.

She stepped closer and pulled a few coppers from her pocket. She was raising her hand to drop them into his bowl when she reconsidered and fished around her pocket for a swan. She didn't want the One God to think she valued her life so lightly.

The silver coin made a dull thunk in the ceramic bowl, and the priest raised his head from his meditations.

"Thank you, my . . . child. I don't get much silver from others around here. May the One God bring down His blessing upon thee!"

The man had been looking down when she'd approached, but had known she'd dropped in a silver. It was the dullness of the silver hitting the bowl. She'd have been able to make the distinction herself. Steel would ring out when you struck it against something. And a tiny copper piece would make a kind of *tick* sound. But even heavy pieces of gold and silver guarded their secrets more closely. Was that why they were stolen? Because they didn't jingle in your pockets the same as other metals? Their duller notes masking their theft?

She shook her head at entertaining such idle thoughts. It wasn't like her to daydream like that. She needed to focus on her problems.

"Father . . . I am here because you've

helped me before, and Huw always told me to go to you if anything ever happened to him. And, well, I can't find him. And . . . the Snart brothers are dead. And if you introduced me to Huw in the first place, and he trusts you, then I figure you must be someone special."

The priest looked up at her. He was old. His hair and beard were white and just a touch wild, and his skin was weathered, but his brown eyes were bright and warm and clear. He was dressed in a simple robe of undyed wool. It was worn at the hem and at the cuffs of its sleeves, but it was surprisingly clean. She supposed he didn't move about much, so maybe there wasn't much occasion to get it dirty.

He spoke up, his voice strong and firm, and younger than his appearance would have suggested. "Oskar. I am sorry about your friends. They were troubled boys. But they were victims long before they were killed last night. I tried to help them over the years. But they resisted my efforts. Perhaps because they had each other, they felt they didn't need anyone else. Foolish notion, that. We all need help now and again."

Oskar had never talked to the Begging Priest at length, only exchanged a few words while she was dropping coins in his bowl.

He continued. "Huw told me you have a

good heart. And while he has tried to teach you what he could and keep you safe, he does not think you are cut out for life on the streets."

Oskar's stomach dropped. "He . . . *what*?"

"He never told you as much, then? He would have soon. I promise you that. We spoke of you often. You always made him proud. You have a bit of the protector in you. Like Huw. And like me. But our fates were sealed long ago. And you are young yet."

Oskar didn't know what to make of the man's speech, but he continued before she could think to offer any kind of response.

"I have a friend down south. He keeps out of politics. I am sure he would take you in. He is a monk—like me. But truly, not like any man of the cloth you have ever met. He believes in teaching the youth of our land. And he judges a man by his deeds, not by his birth. You would be welcome there. And safe."

Oskar waited for him to continue. But this time, he did not. So she queried, "South?"

"Yes. Ridderzaal. Many, many years ago, it was once a capital itself, of a different land than we live in today. It was a place where people fought over ideas. About right and wrong. About justice and goodness. The spirit of that older place lives on in Ridderzaal. And in my friend, Brother Cedric."

Oskar had never heard of Ridderzaal. Not surprising, she supposed. She only knew of the towns immediately surrounding Arlon. And Aoilfhionn, of course. The home of the elves. And . . . a place called Pretania, where Arlon got much of its wool, and another called Laon, where the grain came from for their bread. And some tales of a forest far away where they practiced magic . . .

The Begging Priest continued. "But you will need to take cover for a week or two until I can arrange things. Until then, is there somewhere you can hide where you will feel safe?"

Oskar shook her head. She wasn't sure she'd ever feel safe again. But aloud she answered, "I think so."

13

INTRIGUE'S END

It took all of Oskar's will to climb back up to the roof and wait in her usual spot for Nia to appear that night. At least, she hoped her . . . *friend* would appear. Huw was still missing, and she didn't know who else to turn to. But she would be ready to bolt if she saw so much as the smallest disturbance in her vision, or even a shadow of that man.

This time, Oskar was proud that she noticed Nia approaching from the roof on the opposite side of the alley. Nia moved quickly. Faster than a walk, and more fluid. And when she jumped the alleyway, it was as graceful as a cat stepping over a puddle in the street.

"Did you hear?"

Nia nodded. "I did. And before you ask me any questions . . . I have a confession to make. I was charged with protecting you. And with seeing that the letter you stole was kept safe. Do you have it?"

The letter? Could the Snart brothers have been killed over a letter?

"Y-yes. I have the letter." Oskar absent-mindedly retrieved it from inside her tunic, where it was tucked firmly in place behind her belt. It had bent during her fall, but the vellum was sturdy. And it was essentially unharmed.

Nia took the letter and seemed to relax once she'd tucked it into her own belt.

A thought occurred to Oskar. "But . . . how did you know I was going to steal the letter when you first approached me? The Snart brothers hadn't even . . . *convinced* me to become involved yet."

"Truly coincidence. Or perhaps fate. I did not know our paths would become so entangled when I spoke to you that first time."

Oskar was still too stunned to know how to feel about having to hand the letter over to Nia. "So . . . you and I . . . we are on the same side when it comes to this letter?"

Nia nodded. "Yes. When it became known that the Snart brothers had been engaged to perform the work of retrieving that letter, my patron was concerned they—and you—might fail. I was instructed to ensure that the retrieval was successful. I nearly failed you last night. The man who came after you is known to me. He comes from my homeland. His skills, in magic and otherwise, are . . . significant. And I was following too far behind you to do anything about it. In any event, you should be safe now that I have the letter."

"But how will he know? Won't he keep coming after me?"

"No, I won't." The thickly accented voice came from behind her, on the roof above them both.

Oskar turned around just in time to see the sorcerer's rod reaching toward her—

And then it was gone. Knocked away and spinning silently through the air, out over the rooftops. Nia had thrust one of her daggers into the space between Oskar and the sorcerer, and flipped away the wand. Then she flowed upward and around Oskar as she moved toward their attacker. She spun the blade in her hand and drew a second from her sleeve and plunged them both into the chest of the man before them.

Except that the blades passed right through his body. Nia stumbled and had to recover her balance as the simulacrum dissipated around her. As she looked around for their enemy, the sorcerer materialized behind her and extended his rod—toward Nia this time. The rod grazed her arm as she attempted to dodge, and Nia immediately slumped to the roof as if the bones had left her body.

Without hesitation, the sorcerer stepped over Nia's inert form and extended the rod toward Oskar again. She could smell her attacker this time. His unwashed body, along with a heavy blend of spices. This was no illusion. She fell back onto her bottom and scrabbled up the roof and away from her assailant.

Nia's body shifted slightly and began to slide. As it did, the sorcerer lost his footing and was suddenly struggling to remain upright. His foot had caught in Nia's hood, and as her body tumbled off the roof, the sorcerer was pulled along with her. He didn't even try to stop his fall. But his dark, bloodshot eyes locked on Oskar's for a fraction of a second as he went over the edge. Oskar remained where she was for a moment in disbelief. Then she carefully worked her way down to the roof's edge and looked over. Two bodies, side by side, lay in the alley below.

Oskar made her way to a makeshift ladder at the back side of the building and scrambled down to the ground as fast as she could. Her heart was pounding as she raced toward the alley where Nia and the sorcerer had fallen.

Caution encouraged her to slow down as she turned the corner. But she needn't have worried. Nia and the dark mage were both lying where she'd seen them from above.

They had fallen silently. She had been the only one to bear witness.

Thoughts were swimming in her head.

How could someone as nimble and skilled as Nia be killed so easily? It seemed unjust that a man should be able to defeat her with a simple touch. How out of proportion was the capacity of his magic that it could bring down a young woman who had seemed so powerful? A force of nature. As graceful and perfect in her movement as a cat.

And what now? Should Oskar try to see that Nia was given a proper funeral? How did Nia's people deal with their dead? Would she have been buried? Cremated? And who would she tell about the girl's death? Was her mother even alive?

Oskar noticed the sorcerer's wand lying on the ground near her foot. Her spine quivered, and she took an involuntary step backward.

Then Oskar thought of the letter she'd been tasked with stealing. Should she retrieve it? She looked at the fallen body of . . . *her friend* . . . Nia's eyes were closed. And she looked as though she could have been sleeping. Oskar decided that she didn't have the heart to retrieve the letter, or solve the mystery of what to do with Nia's body.

Be practical. Think of yourself first. Don't allow yourself to feel compassion or sorrow for others. Or it will be your downfall! That was what Huw would have told her. So she straightened herself up as best she could and walked slowly away. She would find Huw and tell him she was leaving, that the Begging Priest had already arranged for her to go somewhere safe.

She glanced back once at her friend lying on the alley floor. There was nothing she could do for Nia now. The girl who dealt with death had finally come face-to-face with her master.

14

NO GOODBYES

Over the next several days, Oskar could find no trace of Huw. She returned once to the alley where Nia and the dark mage had fallen, and discovered that their bodies were gone. When she checked in with some of Huw's whisperers, they had heard nothing. It was as if the shadow walker and her killer had never existed. Only Oskar seemed to know anything about either one of them.

She returned to the Begging Priest several times, always in the morning, after sleeping in a different hole every night. He gave her food and water. And they spoke.

Of Huw—and how the priest thought he might still live, since they had not yet found his body. Of how Huw would have let himself be found if he had wanted to, or thought it was safe. And of how he would want Oskar to leave Arlon regardless. It still stung, however. When she let herself think of it for what it was. Yes, she understood that he might have been looking out for himself and his own safety. But if he was alive, and well, then that meant he had abandoned her. At a time when she needed him most.

They talked of the Snart brothers, for whom Oskar suddenly found herself feeling some compassion for the first time in her life. They had had nobody else but each other in all the world. At least Oskar had had Huw. And, so very briefly, Nia.

The priest told her of Ridderzaal and what she could expect there.

But they never spoke of the sorcerer. And never of Nia. If the priest knew of those details in Oskar's story, he never made it known. And he was kind enough to avoid speaking of them if he did.

It was nearly two weeks after Nia was killed by dark magic that Oskar left Arlon.

The journey would take about a week, walking beside a merchant's cart along with a handful of priests who wanted to study the famed religious scrolls at Ridderzaal's monastery. Her elbow was still sore, but she had left her sling behind. And while her legs and hips were mostly recovered, she found that she actually welcomed the promise of a slow pace.

As Oskar made her way beyond the southern gates of the city with her discretion of priests, the day was crisp with the promise of the coming fall. The familiar smells of the city began to fade behind her. And as they walked farther into the countryside, she began to notice new smells—of the plants and the surrounding woods.

She was so overcome by the fragrances she took in with every breath that she stopped to pick up a handful of dirt. Ignoring the raised eyebrows of the priest walking beside her, she raised it to her nose and inhaled deeply. Even the dirt smelled clean beyond the city walls.

EPILOGUE

A covered walkway extended from the
western face of the monastery to a
postern gate at the left rear corner of Ridderzaal Castle. To the left of a large double-
doored entrance on the northeastern face of
the monastery was a small footpath that led
to one of the outbuildings and its much
smaller and humbler door. Gathered around
the door were three boys.

Two boys stood to one side, talking together in low voices. One was tall and broad
of chest. Oskar's breath caught in her throat
at the sight of him. What a figure he cut! She
had to force herself to keep walking. But she
couldn't avoid a slight hitch in her gait as she
recovered. The other boy with him was
shorter and slighter of build, and he leaned
nonchalantly against a low railing. He saw

her approaching and offered her a dazzling smile. "Good morning!"

Oh my. If these were her fellow students, she should have left Arlon sooner.

She had begun to smile in return when she noticed the glare of the third boy. He was shorter than the first and stockier than the second. But his face bore a look that could have soured milk. He ran his eyes up and down her lanky frame, and his face distorted from a sneer of anger into one of disgust. "Tell me this peasant isn't going to be studying with us."

Oskar knew his type. A prickly and entitled noble. If she was any judge, he was toothless, and he used his bark to try to scare away the easily cowed. But she didn't know who might be watching from one of the monastery windows, or if this might be some kind of test. So she said nothing and stepped off to the side to wait by herself. If a spoiled-brat nobleman's son was the worse she would face down here, she'd call it a fair trade for what she had left behind.

ALSO BY MATTHEW B. BERG

Available Now!

A Monk's Tale - The first novelette released in the world of The Crafter Chronicles

The Crafter's Son - Book One of the Exciting New Coming of Age Epic Fantasy Series, The Crafter Chronicles

The Queen & The Soldier - Book Two of the Exciting New Coming of Age Epic Fantasy Series, The Crafter Chronicles

The Cat's Paw - Another novelette in the world of The Crafter Chronicles

Coming in 2021 . . .

The Ranger King - Book Three of the Exciting New Coming of Age Epic Fantasy Series, The Crafter Chronicles (Also the *concluding* volume in the series trilogy!)

The Lay of Legorel (working title) - Yet another novelette in the world of The Crafter Chronicles

A BRIEF GLOSSARY, WITH PRONUNCIATIONS

Aoilfhionn - *(Ā-ō-lǝn)* - *The city of trees. Capital city of Fardach Sidhe, homeland of the elves.*

Arlon - *(ar-LON)* - *The capital of Hyrde, and seat of the kingdom.*

(The) Begging Priest - *A mendicant cleric who lives on the streets of Arlon and helps those in need.*

Erda - *(UR-dä)* - *The continent of known lands where* The Crafter's Chronicles *takes place.*

Hugo - *(HYOO-go)* - *The younger, and much larger, of the infamous Snart brothers.*

Huw - *(HYOO) - A merchant thief from Arlon.*

Laon - *(LAY-on) - The breadbasket of Erda. A flat land of rich soil where a majority of the grain consumed in Erda is produced. Occupying the southwest corner of Erda, between the forests of Fardach Sidhe and Shenn Frith, and the swamplands of Geornlice.*

Mirgul - *(MEER-gül) - A god. Brother to Mirren.*

Mirren - *(MIR-en) - A god. Brother to Mirgul.*

Mungo - *(Mung-go) - Pretani god of luck.*

Namur - *(NÄ-mur) - A land of rolling hills and wild grassland where the Namur people raise their herds of half-tame horses. It occupies the region between Pretania to the west, Krigsrike to the north, Ath to the east, and Hyrde to the south.*

Nia - *(NEE-ah) - A mysterious*

and dangerous woman from
Namur.

Oskar - *(AWE-skər)* - *An orphan,
from the streets of Arlon.*

Pretania - *(pre-TÄN-ya)* - *A land
of high elevation with a
challenging terrain composed
of bluffs and steep hills,
occupying the northwest
region of Erda.*

Pretani/Pretanian - *(pre-TÄN-
ē/pre-TÄN-ē-ən)* - *The people
of Pretania.*

Riderzaal *(RID-ur-zäl)* - *The
name of the castle, and the
city which surrounds it, in the
south of Hyrde, on Long Lake.*

Wymar - *(WHY-mar)* - *The
older, and shorter, of the
infamous Snart brothers.*

* *Stress/emphasis is shown by
word parts in ALL CAPS
(non-stressed syllables are in
lower case). Where I've used
symbols or diacritical marks,
here is what they mean!*

a - *"a" as in* bad

ä- *"ah" as in* ma *or* father
ā - *"ay" as in* day
ə - *"uh" as in* duh *or* what
e - *"e" as in* bed
ē- *"ee" as in* feed
i - *"ih" as in* dip
ī– *"ii" as in* wide
ʒ - *"zh" as in* version *or* usual
ö - *"oe" as in* voyeur
ō- *"oh" as in* go
ü- *"oo" as in* goose *or* blue

Other:

Knight-Captain - *A commanding officer of an army of knights and accompanying foot soldiers.*

Knight-General - *A commanding officer in charge of a nation's army in times of war.*

Currency:
1 gold crown = 10 silver swans
1 silver swan = 10 copper commons

Join the Crafter's Guild!

This book may have ended. But your journey begins now.

Join the guild and become part of the story.

- Members of the guild are always the first to hear about Matthew's new books and publications.
- Members will receive access to free behind-the-scenes content.
- Finally, some lucky guild members will have the opportunity to become beta readers for book three!

Join the Crafter's Guild!
http://www.matthewbberg.com/join

Reviews needed!

Like the book? If so, it would mean a lot to me if you would leave a review on Amazon or Goodreads.

Many people won't gamble on a new writer. So the more positive reviews I can accumulate, the more likely it is for other readers to give my work a chance.

Thanks in advance for your help!

ABOUT THE AUTHOR

Matthew Berg is a Director of IT by day, a dad and husband by night and weekend, and a writer by commute. He loves to travel—though mostly for the food. He's been playing D&D (on and off) since he and his brothers picked up the *Basic Set* at Lauriat's Books in 1977. He is known to attend renaissance fairs in period garb. And he has far, far too many hobbies.

Since he is just getting started he doesn't have compelling quotes about his work to share from authors like Terry Brooks and Brandon Sanderson. Yet. But when he does, you can be sure he'll include them here in his author's biography.